GEARING UP

© 2011 MATTEL, INC. ALL RIGHTS RESERVED.
978-0-00-742666-9
1 3 5 7 9 10 8 6 4 2
First published in the UK by HarperCollins Children's Books in 2011

A CIP catalogue record for this title is available from the British Library.

www.harpercollins.co.uk

Printed and bound in China

HarperCollins *Children's Books*

Battle Force 5 were on their first mission. As they accelerated towards the stormshock, the wheels on their vehicles glowed red.

'I've got some hot wheels!' Zoom cried. He pulled a wheelie and snuck ahead of the rest of the team. 'We have lift off!' Sherman shouted as their vehicles were taken up into the stormshock by the winds.

A hologram of Sage appeared on Vert's dashboard. 'You will soon be out of radio contact. Remember, you must secure the battle key.'

'We're on it, Sage,' Vert assured her.

'The portal's open, floor it!' Vert ordered.

'The enemy will be waiting on the other side. Get ready to crash and bash!' They hurtled through the portal.

They shot out of the portal into a battle zone that looked like the inner workings of a clock. They screeched to a halt and stared around in disbelief. 'This is a battle zone?' Zoom gasped.

'Get the battle key, get out of the zone and lock it down,' Vert told them.

Agura was staring at an object floating just ahead of them. 'I'm guessing that's the battle key?' she asked. But Zoom had spotted something else. Another portal was opening. Four vehicles shot through the portal.

'Captain Kalus and his Vandals,' Vert said in a low voice. But another portal was opening to the right.

'The Sark!' Vert cried as he caught sight of Zemerik.

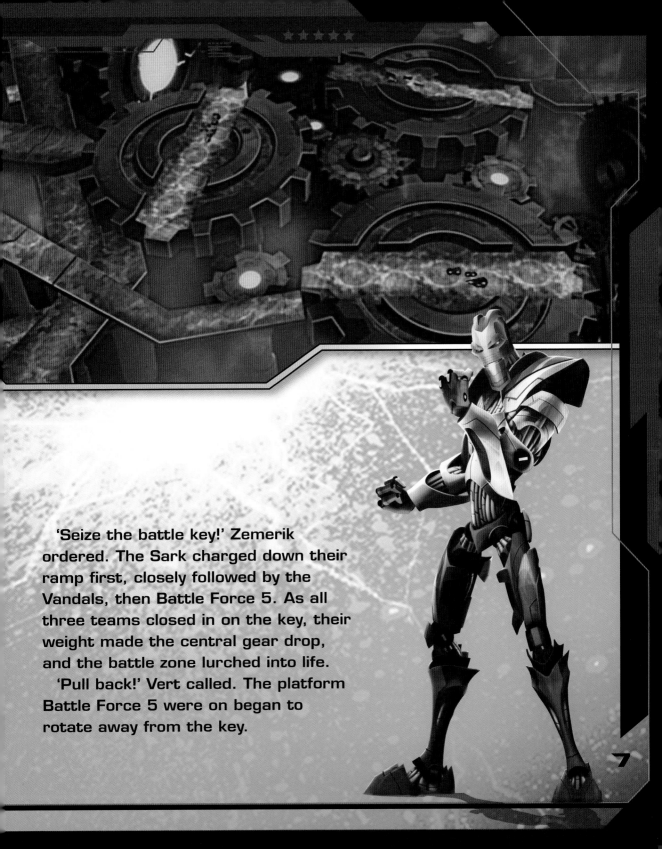

'Seize the battle key!' Zemerik ordered. The Sark charged down their ramp first, closely followed by the Vandals, then Battle Force 5. As all three teams closed in on the key, their weight made the central gear drop, and the battle zone lurched into life.

'Pull back!' Vert called. The platform Battle Force 5 were on began to rotate away from the key.

'Keep your eyes on that key!' Vert ordered. The battle key had started to move away, too. The platforms stopped in their new positions, and the teams hit their accelerators, all blasting towards the key's new location.

Zoom sped up ramp after ramp until he was face to face with a handful of Sark. He rode up an angled cog and flew through the air, the Chopper's wheels splitting into spinning blades. He looked down, realising he was descending towards spinning gears. He hit another cog, ricocheting off it before coming to a stop.

Meanwhile, the Vandals were racing towards Agura. She shot a grapple at Kalus, but he deflected it with ease, then fired a crossbow at her, which sent the Tangler swerving out of control. Agura tried the grapple again, but it caught in a cog mechanism and she was pulled upwards. The Tangler fell, and Agura landed hard, but unhurt.

The Vandals watched Agura speed away on a lower level where she was closer to the key. Kalus roared in fury.

Meanwhile Zug, Zemerik's second-in-command, rammed his Zendrill into the back of the Buster. Spinner frantically pushed every button in the back seat, looking for a weapon. Finally, a mace shot out, but the Zendrill dodged it. Spinner hit another button that deployed a ramp. The Zendrill drove right up the ramp and shot into the air, crash landing in a gear.

Above them, the Vandal Krocomodo tried to snag Stanford's Reverb with the barbed edges of his Riptile. Stanford bounced the Reverb into the air. The barbed edges landed in a spinning gear and pulled the Riptile upwards.

'I've got the key in my sights!' Agura said. She walked the Tangler over the cogs in the gear, then leaped and snagged the key.

'Everybody back to the portal,' Vert ordered. Suddenly, Zemerik manoeuvred his vehicle so that he was blocking their path.

'Organic! You cannot win!' Zemerik warned.

Vert deployed his chainsaw and turned to face Zemerik. Above, Stanford aimed his guns at Zemerik. Vert charged at Zemerik, but at the same time Stanford blasted a sonic boom from his Twin Guns. It hit the Saber, and Vert skidded into the machinery below. The Saber fell and fell until it hit something invisible. The cloaking shield flickered, revealing an enormous vehicle, and the Saber bounced off it and came to rest on the ground.

The Chopper, Buster and Tangler sped down a stretch of road. 'Vert! I found another way down,' Zoom shouted.

Vert was holding his head. 'I'm sorry, mate,' Stanford called. 'What's that?' he added.

'It's a Mobi!' Vert said in disbelief.

'What is a…' Stanford trailed off as the Mobi's cloaking shield flickered back into action. '…WAS a Mobi?' he finished.

Zemerik was speeding down a stretch of road. Suddenly, Kalus appeared from out of nowhere. He pulled alongside Zemerik and shot a damaged area on the Zelix's wheels with a bolt from his crossbow. The Zelix veered off and hit a wall. 'Sark. Retreat. We must prepare a new plan for the destruction of Earth!' Zemerik ordered.

   Back on the lower level, Vert and Stanford were trying to locate
the invisible Mobi. The Tangler, Buster and Chopper approached.
Agura eyed Vert and Stanford quizzically. Vert explained that they
had seen a Mobius Command Centre – a gigantic mobile garage.
'Sage needs it to stay alive. Like cyber life-support,' Vert finished.
   Stanford suddenly hit the shield. He knocked on it triumphantly.
   Spinner pointed to a nearby ramp. The Vandals were descending.
   'We'll come back for the Mobi. Burn rubber for the portal!' shouted
Vert. They tore off, but Kalus hadn't moved. 'Fall back and regroup!'
he ordered.
   'I've found something quite rare.' He smiled as the cloak on the
Mobi flickered, revealing its hiding place.

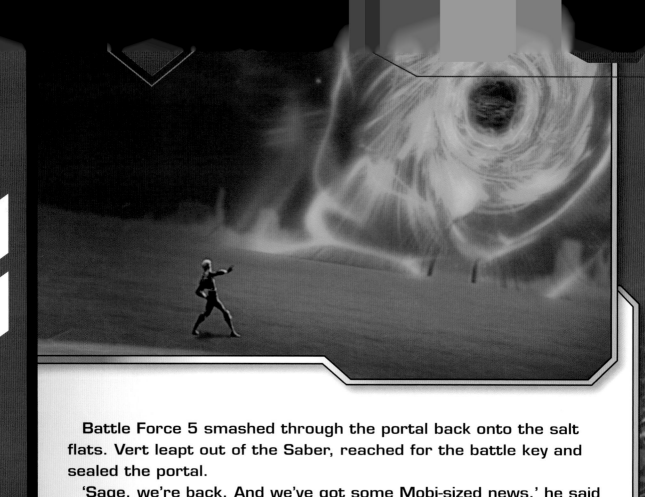

Battle Force 5 smashed through the portal back onto the salt flats. Vert leapt out of the Saber, reached for the battle key and sealed the portal.

'Sage, we're back. And we've got some Mobi-sized news,' he said into his wrist communicator.

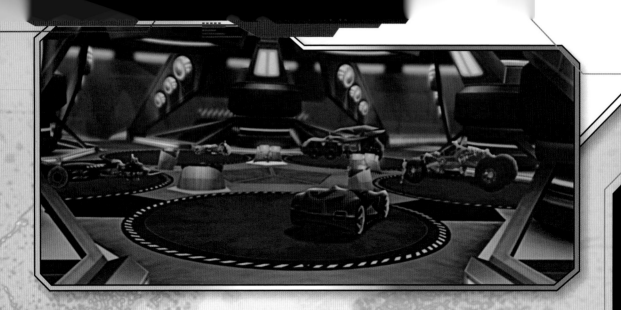

Later that night the team were carrying out repairs on their damaged vehicles.

Sage oversaw their work. Her energy was diminished, and her visible circuitry was flickering.

'You did acquire the battle key,' she said. 'And locating a Mobius Command Centre was an extraordinary accomplishment. Its technology...could provide our enemies...with an enormous advantage,' she finished, falling to her knees. Vert rushed to steady her. The others looked worried.

'The Mobi is Sage's only power source,' Vert explained. 'We've got to get back to that battle zone, and fast.'

Back in their vehicles, Battle Force 5 sped along the salt flats.

'The Mobius Command Centre has an encrypted ignition code,' Sage said.

Vert looked confused.

'A password. So nobody can start the engine without it,' Sherman explained.

Sage whispered, 'Ignition code...first five prime numbers.'

'Two, three, five, seven and eleven. Got it!' Sherman replied.

Sage groaned. 'Entering hibernation mode to protect me during portal crossing.' She transformed into cube form. The battle key magnetically lifted off the Saber and

activated the stormshock.

'Now let's get in there, get that Mobi, and get out of there, FAST!' Vert shouted as Battle Force 5 raced through the portal. Once on the other side, they saw no sign of their enemies.

'The Mobi should be down there, on that gear,' Spinner said.

Stanford blasted his twin guns. The sound waves disrupted the Mobi's shield, and it decloaked. The door at the back opened automatically. Vert looked suspicious. 'Something doesn't feel right,' he said to the others. 'Agura, you and Stanford stay here with Sage and the key. Sherman, Spinner, Zoom, let's check it out.'

The Saber, Chopper and Buster approached the Mobi. Battle Force 5 got out of their vehicles. 'Let's get to the control room,' Vert said. Suddenly, they heard a hissing behind them. They span around – Krocomodo and Hatch stood facing them, smiling. Zoom pulled into a roundhouse kick and hit Krocomodo right in the nose, but Krocomodo beat him away. Suddenly, Kalus leapt off the catwalk above and landed in front of them, snarling. He swiped at them, sending them sprawling backwards. Sever put a restraint around Vert's neck and hands.

'Struggle all you like,' Kalus sneered. 'When I return to Vandal with the Mobi, we will be the most powerful force in the multiverse!'

The Vandals put the other three members of Battle Force 5 in one large restraint.

Agura and Stanford were still waiting outside the Mobi. 'I'm getting a bad feeling about this,' Agura said. 'They've been gone a long time. We should go in.'

'Agura, we can't. Vert gave us an order. If the Vandals get the key, Earth is toast!' Stanford picked Sage up in her cube form and shook her. 'Sage, wake up. We need your advice!' Sage materialised in full form, exhausted.

Back in the Mobi, Kalus was getting frustrated with the controls. 'This Sentient vehicle is useless without the code!' he roared, slamming his fist against the screen. Vert smiled.

Klaus leapt down from the upper level. 'Unlock the vehicle, or your friends will pay!' he snarled.

Stanford, Agura and Sage were looking down at the Mobi. Sage activated a holographic view screen. It gave an infra red view of everybody inside. 'Looks like our guys are in trouble!' Stanford said.

'Since I am the last expert in the workings of the Mobius Command Centre, Kalus will trade his hostages for me,' Sage said.

Back inside the Mobi, Vert was stalling for time. 'Useless sub-creature!' Kalus yelled. 'Why isn't the Mobius moving?'

'I'm human, not Sentient. Their computers don't come with tech help.'

Spinner, Sherman and Zoom chuckled.

'Silence!' Kalus roared.

Sage, still flickering, rode a giant cog down to the Mobi.
'Captain Kalus, this is Sage,' she said into her wrist communicator.
'Speak your business, Sentient,' he growled.
'Free the Earthlings and in return, I offer myself. And my vast technical knowledge.'

Kalus rode out to meet Sage, Agura and Stanford.
Suddenly, Kalus whipped out his bolo-weapon and lassoed Sage, yanking her aboard his chariot.

'Negotiations have taken a new twist,' Kalus sneered, before speeding off. Agura began to give chase, but the other Vandals blocked her. Sever activated the rotating teeth of his Water Slaughter. Stanford pulled out his twin guns and blasted the Water Slaughter to the edge of the platform. Krocomodo charged at the Tangler, but Agura extended its legs so it rose into the air, then brought it down hard, crushing the vehicles.

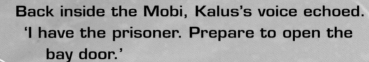

Back inside the Mobi, Kalus's voice echoed. 'I have the prisoner. Prepare to open the bay door.'

As Hatch went to open the door, Vert entered the prime numbers into the control panel. The command centre's monitors blinked to life and the engines hummed. Vert aimed a kick straight at Hatch's face, sending him flying, then jumped after him, hitting the button to free the others. Once free, Spinner turned the key in Vert's restraint.

Hatch charged at Spinner, but Spinner dodged out of the way and he slammed into the ramp release button on the wall. The ramp descended. Sherman and Spinner pushed Hatch down the ramp and out of the Mobi.

'Kalus has Sage!' Agura called. 'And it looks like he's heading back towards Vandal.'

'I've got an idea,' Vert told her. The Mobi screeched to a halt and Vert flipped the front hatch open. 'Spinner, fire up the Mobi's vehicle accelerator,' he ordered. 'Sherman, figure out the calculations to fire the Saber and the Chopper together. Zoom, gear up. You're about to do zero to sixty in no time flat.'

Back in the battle zone, a portal opened and the Fangore, Kalus's chariot, approached, with Sage huddled in the back.

'OK Vert, I've used the vehicles' weight and distance to calculate the acceleration. You'll hit your target,' Sherman confirmed.
Zoom smiled. 'Let's do this!'
Spinner hit a button on the control panel. The Saber shot out of the back hatch, closely followed by the Chopper. The Saber flew over Kalus, and landed between him and the portal, whilst Zoom drifted in behind him. Kalus roared as both Vert and Zoom charged at him. They collided, flipping Kalus's vehicle into the air and Sage flew out. Zoom launched the Chopper into the air and caught her, then sped back to the Mobi.

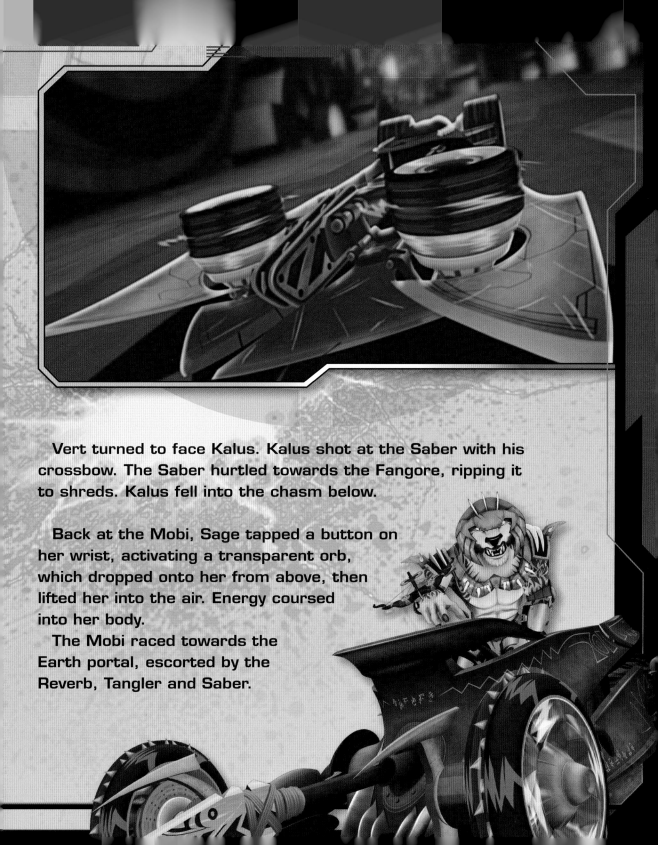

Vert turned to face Kalus. Kalus shot at the Saber with his crossbow. The Saber hurtled towards the Fangore, ripping it to shreds. Kalus fell into the chasm below.

Back at the Mobi, Sage tapped a button on her wrist, activating a transparent orb, which dropped onto her from above, then lifted her into the air. Energy coursed into her body.

The Mobi raced towards the Earth portal, escorted by the Reverb, Tangler and Saber.

Kalus had pulled himself back up to the ledge. He jumped on the Mobi as it drove past. Battle Force 5 hurtled through the portal.

Vert pulled alongside the Mobi and jumped on to the top of the vehicle, brandishing a sword.

He threw a few wide swings, forcing Kalus to topple into an opening. Vert dropped down beside him, his sword pointed at Kalus's neck. Sage was now back to full power. She stared down at Kalus, then hit a button on the console beside her. Energy gathered behind Kalus, and before he knew what was happening he shot out of the vehicle.

He flew across the desert and right into the stormshock, where Agura was waiting to close the portal.

Back in the Mobi, Battle Force 5 were celebrating.

'Vert, dude, you were awesome!' Zoom laughed.

'Thanks, but it was a team victory, guys. We all won this!'

'On this mission, defeat is not an option,' Sage told them.
'No matter how many times you are tested, or how terrifying
the test.'

'And we're up for it. Right?' Vert turned to the rest of the
team.

He raised his fist in the air, and the others joined him.

'Battle Force 5!' they shouted together.

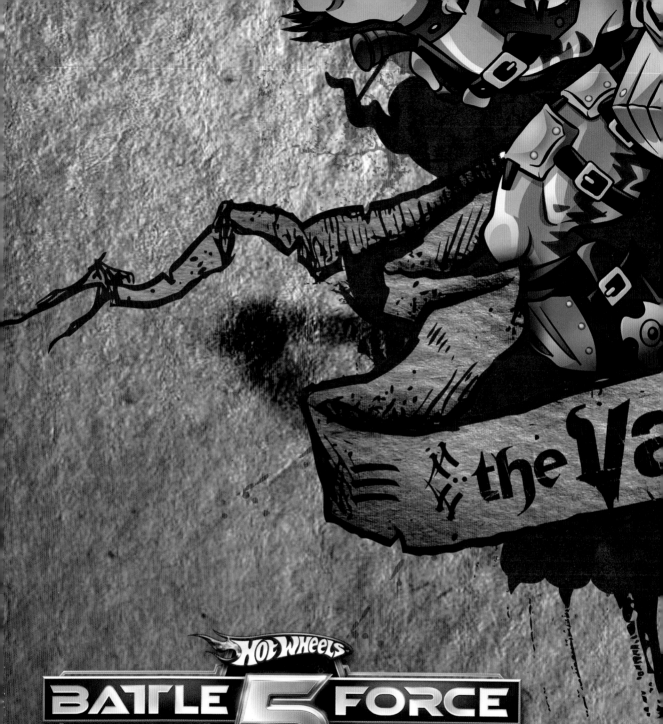

the Va

HOT WHEELS

BATTLE 5 FORCE